Thank You and Good Night

Patrick McDonnell

LB

LITTLE, BROWN AND COMPANY
NEW YORK   BOSTON

Little, Brown and Company

Hachette Book Group
1290 Avenue of the Americas, New York, NY 10104
Visit us at lb-kids.com

Little, Brown and Company is a division of Hachette Book Group, Inc.
The Little, Brown name and logo are trademarks of Hachette Book Group, Inc.

The publisher is not responsible for websites (or their content) that are not owned by the publisher.

First Edition: October 2015

Library of Congress Cataloging-in-Publication Data

McDonnell, Patrick, 1956– author, illustrator.
Thank you and good night / Patrick McDonnell. — First edition.
pages cm
Summary: Maggie hosts a pajama party at which Clement, Alan Alexander, and Jean play a variety of fun games,
tire themselves, and drift off to sleep, but not before sharing their gratitude.
ISBN 978-0-316-33801-1 (hardcover)
[1. Sleepovers—Fiction. 2. Friendship—Fiction. 3. Bedtime—Fiction. 4. Gratitude—Fiction.] I. Title.
PZ7.M1554Th 2015
[E]—dc23
2014035293

10 9 8 7 6 5 4 3 2 1

SC

PRINTED IN CHINA

This book was edited by Andrea Spooner and designed by Jeff Schulz and Patrick McDonnell with art direction
by Patti Ann Harris. The production was supervised by Erika Schwartz, and the production editor was Barbara Bakowski.
The illustrations for this book were done in pen and ink, pencil, and watercolor on handmade paper.
The text was set in Celestia Antiqua Std, and the display type is St. Nicholas.

The sun set,
the moon rose,

and Maggie helped Clement
button his favorite pajamas—
the ones with the blue and white stripes.

"We're here!" announced Jean
and his friend Alan Alexander.

Jean's pajamas had feet in them.
Alan's pajamas seemed a little too big.

"Surprise!" said Maggie.

"Wheeee!" said Jean.

"Hooray!" said Clement.

"Oops!" said Alan.

"Now what?" Jean wondered.

"Is it time for bed?" Clement asked.

"No," Alan declared.

Alan taught the chicken dance.

Clement won the funny-face contest.

The three friends played hide-and-seek,

again and again.

"Is it time for bed yet?" asked Clement.

"No, no, no," Alan replied.

They bounced the balloon about,

practiced yoga,

and had a little something good to eat.

They studied the night sky,

saw a shooting star,

and made a wish.

A night bird sang a lullaby.

"Sweet sleep,
Sweet sleep,
Sweet sleep."

"Gee, I'm getting sleepy." Jean sighed.

"Gee, I'm getting sleepier," Alan mumbled.

"Gee, I'm already asleep." Clement yawned.

"Now is it time for bed?" they all asked quietly.

"Yes," said Maggie.

Everyone got ready.

They sleepwalked down the hall…

…and snuggled under the blankets.
"Will you tell us a story?" they asked.

"Once upon a time…" Maggie started.

"Ooh, that's a good one!" exclaimed Alan Alexander.

"Hush," whispered Clement.

Maggie read them their favorite bedtime stories—

stories about a majestic elephant,
a brave bear,
and a quiet bunny....

Stories that bring sweet dreams.

"Now, before we go to sleep, let's all say
what we were thankful for this day."

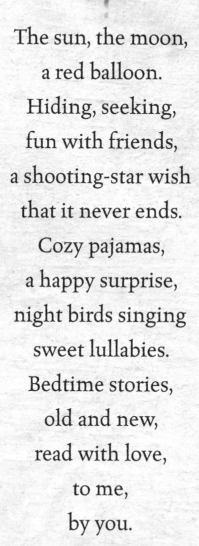

The sun, the moon,
a red balloon.
Hiding, seeking,
fun with friends,
a shooting-star wish
that it never ends.
Cozy pajamas,
a happy surprise,
night birds singing
sweet lullabies.
Bedtime stories,
old and new,
read with love,
to me,
by you.

A long, long list
of that and this,
ending with
a good-night kiss.

"Thank you."

"Thank you."

"Thank you."

And good night.